Merry Un Christmas

For Ian Abrams
—M.R.

To the fuzzy brothers
—D.C.

Merry Un-Christmas

Text copyright © 2006 by Mike Reiss   Illustrations copyright © 2006 by David Catrow   Manufactured in China.   All rights
reserved. No part of this book may be used or reproduced in any manner whatsoever without written permission except in the case of brief
quotations embodied in critical articles and reviews. For information address HarperCollins Children's Books, a division of HarperCollins
Publishers, 1350 Avenue of the Americas, New York, NY 10019.   www.harpercollinschildrens.com   Library of Congress Cataloging-
in-Publication Data   Reiss, Mike.   Merry un-Christmas / by Mike Reiss ; illustrated by David Catrow.— 1st ed.   p. cm.   Summary:
Noelle celebrates the only day in Christmas City that is not Christmas, by undecorating the tree, greeting the postman, and going to school.
ISBN-10: 0-06-059126-9 (trade bdg.) — ISBN-13: 978-0-06-059126-7 (trade bdg.)   ISBN-10: 0-06-059127-7 (lib. bdg.) —
ISBN-13: 978-0-06-059127-4 (lib. bdg.)   [1. Christmas—Fiction.] I. Catrow, David, ill. II. Title.   PZ7.R2784Mer 2006
2005022736 [E]—dc22   CIP   AC   Typography by Elynn Cohen   1 2 3 4 5 6 7 8 9 10   ❖   First Edition

Merry Un Christmas

By Mike Reiss • Illustrated by David Catrow

HarperCollins*Publishers*

It was Christmas morning, and Noelle was opening her presents. She got a new doll, a dollhouse, ice skates, roller skates, a computer, and a bike. Oh yes, and a pony.

"Gee, thanks," she said with a yawn.

Noelle put her bike in the garage with all her other bikes . . .
and let her pony play in the backyard with all her
other ponies.

For Christmas dinner, Noelle's mother made turkey with chestnut dressing and mashed potatoes and carrots and peas and five kinds of pie.

"Turkey with chestnut dressing and mashed potatoes and carrots
and peas and five kinds of pie *again*?" her father moaned.
Noelle ate exactly three peas and excused herself.

Noelle squeezed into her room through all the dolls and skates and computers. "Another boring day," she said with a sigh, and went to sleep. And when she woke up the next morning . . .

it was Christmas again.
"Nuts," thought Noelle.

Now, don't think that Noelle is a spoiled brat or that her family is crazy. They're all very nice people, I assure you. It's just that they live in Christmas City, in the state of Texmas. It's the one place in the world where it's Christmas 364 days a year.

That night Noelle's father was reading the newspaper. Noelle saw something on the back page that made her heart dance with joy. It was an ad that said:

ONLY 3 MORE NONSHOPPING DAYS TILL UN-CHRISTMAS

"Is it true?" Noelle gasped.

"Check the calendar," her mother said with a smile.

It was true! Soon it would be Un-Christmas, the one unmagical nonholiday in Christmas City. Everyone loved Un-Christmas, but no one loved it more than Noelle.

The family set to work getting ready for Un-Christmas. They undecorated the Christmas tree and took the wreath off the front door. When Father took the tree out to the street, Noelle couldn't believe how big and empty the living room looked.

"It's beautiful," she said.

Noelle was up bright and early on Un-Christmas morning. She was so excited. She didn't have to unwrap any presents or pose for any pictures! She didn't have to kiss her uncle Dave with the beard or aunt Polly with the mustache! But there was one thing she did have to do.... She had to go to school!

Since schools are closed for Christmas, Noelle's school was open only one day a year: Un-Christmas Day. It was great fun for Noelle to be in one big room with all her friends: Christine, Kris, Chrissy, Holly, Carol, Christopher, Noel, and Claus.

All the kids in Christmas City *loved* school.

Don't you?

After school, Noelle went home and turned on the TV. There were no holiday specials, no Christmas parades, no Grinch, and no Scrooge. She got to see all new shows: cartoons and soap operas and *Oprah* and something wonderful called *Gilligan's Island*.

Noelle thought nothing could tear her away from the TV. But
then she caught sight of a chubby man with a sack—a man who
came to visit just once a year....

It was the mailman!

Since the post office is closed on Christmas, this was the only day he could bring mail. As the mailman emptied out his sack, Noelle sang her favorite Un-Christmas carol:

There's nobody merrier
Than the letter carrier
With the biggest bag you've ever seen.
Filled with lots of bills for Dad
(Cheer up, Father, don't be mad!)
Postcards, junk mail, and some magazines!

"Guess what we're having for Un-Christmas dinner," said Noelle's mother.

"Meatloaf?" said Noelle's father hopefully.

"Leftovers?" said Noelle, licking her lips.

"Even better," said her mother. "We're having TV dinners!"

And everyone cheered.

After Un-Christmas dinner, Noelle and her parents
went downtown for the traditional de-lighting of
the Christmas tree. The Mayor of Christmas
City threw a giant switch, and every light
on the giant evergreen tree went out.
It was so dark that people could
see thousands of stars twinkling
in the sky. "Oooooh," said
the crowd.

"De-lightful," Noelle's father said every year. His dumb joke
was a tradition, too.

As her mother tucked her into bed, Noelle said, "I wish it could be Un-Christmas every day."

"Oh, I bet you'd get tired of it after a while," said her mother.

"I bet I wouldn't," said Noelle before she drifted off to a most perfect sleep.